See additional verses inside.

The Jungle

Baseball Game

BY
Tom Paxton

ILLUSTRATED BY
Karen Lee Schmidt

MORROW JUNIOR BOOKS · New York

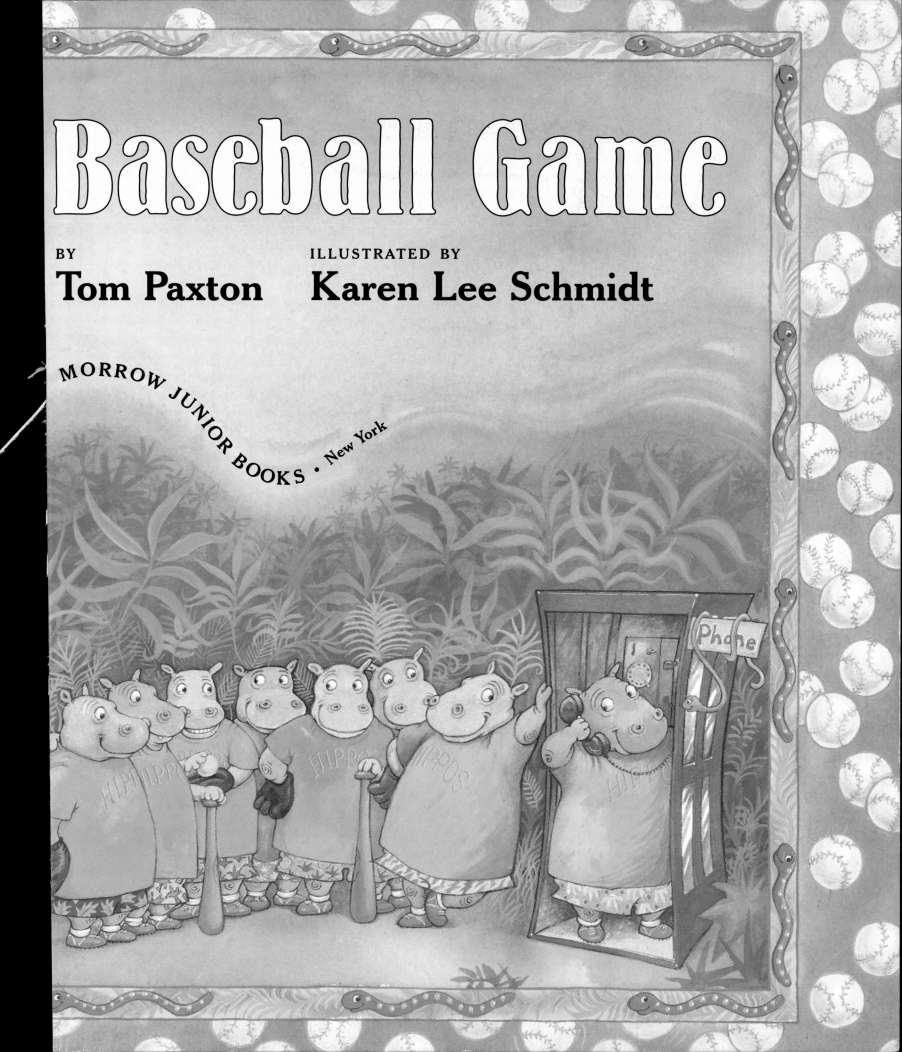

Watercolor and gouache were used for the full-color illustrations.
The text type is 20-point Cheltenham.

Text copyright © 1999 by Pax Music, ASCAP
Illustrations copyright © 1999 by Karen Lee Schmidt

Published by Morrow Junior Books, a division of William Morrow and Company, Inc.,
1350 Avenue of the Americas, New York, NY 10019.

Printed in Singapore at Tien Wah Press.

1 2 3 4 5 6 7 8 9 10

Library of Congress Cataloging-in-Publication Data
Paxton, Tom.
The jungle baseball game/by Tom Paxton; illustrated by Karen Lee Schmidt.
p. cm.
Summary: The jungle animals enjoy a rousing game of baseball.
ISBN 0-688-13979-5 (trade)—ISBN 0-688-13980-9 (library)
[1. Jungle animals—Fiction.   2. Baseball—Fiction.]   I. Schmidt, Karen, ill.
II. Title.   PZ8.3.P2738Ju 1999   [E]—dc21   97-6459   CIP AC

To Petey and Daisy Landi,
in honor of their grandfather and my friend
Peter Dohanos
—T.P.

To my aunt Clara H. Brown,
for friendship and early morning waffles
—K.L.S.

Rang-alang-lang, the telephone rang,
Way up in the coconut tree.
Mister Monkey ran to answer—
"Someone's calling me."
Mister Hippo, on the line,
Yelled, "Am I getting through?
Get your monkey baseball team—
We want to play ball with you."

When the monkeys saw the hippos,
All they did was laugh.
"Those slowpokes should just be glad
To get our autograph!"

Watching the hippos warming up,
They laughed themselves to tears.
Jumping round the dugout,
They led their fans in cheers:

"Whacka, whacka, hoo boy,
Tie 'em with a rope.

Poor old hippos
Haven't got a hope!"

A chimpanzee played out in left;
A baboon stood in right.
The orangutan on the pitcher's mound
Was a most impressive sight.

Little monkeys in the field
Were the quickest ones of all.
Far as the hippos hit the pitch,
Those monkeys caught the ball.

As they watched the monkeys play,
The challengers were glum.
They could *never* lick the champs;
The hippos felt so dumb.
Missing pitches, dropping fly balls,
Tripping over feet,
Nervously they thought about
The team they could not beat.

On and on the monkeys laughed,
Though no one scored a run.
Inning after inning,
They just played for fun.

Their fans were up and shouting;
Creatures whooped and cheered.
They gobbled up the hot dogs
As the popcorn disappeared.

The monkeys went on jeering
Till the hippos cried, "Enough!"
Grimly they played harder
And vowed to show their stuff.

They all buckled down and so,
In spite of their great weight,
They played so well that not one
Prancing monkey crossed the plate.

Now the hippos swung their bats
As if they meant to win,
Thundering around the bases
While their fans began to grin.

The monkeys stared in wonder.
They'd never been outdone.
Till, all at once, with four base hits,
The hippos scored a run!

The monkeys knew they had to score
Or kiss the game good-bye.
It was now the bottom of the ninth,
Time for do or die.
First, the chimpanzee struck out;
"Strike three!" the orangutan heard.
Then a baboon got a hit
And ran all the way to third.

Now the monkeys saw their chance;
Their hopes began to rise.
Finally they saw the way
To beat those tubby guys.
Still, the monkeys had two outs;
Their manager chewed his hat.
He could hardly bear to look
As the gorilla came to bat.

The gorilla stepped up to the plate
And took a practice swing.
His bat looked like a tree trunk
When he twirled it like a sling.
Then the pitcher wound up,
And a perfect curve she threw.
"Strike one!" called the umpire,
And the next pitch was "Strike two!"

First the windup, then the pitch,
Then a splitting *crack*!
Up, up, up the baseball soared.
Would it ever be coming back?

Every anxious pair of eyes
Searched the cloudless sky.
No one there had ever seen
A baseball fly so high.

When the ball headed back toward earth,
A wind came from the north.
It tossed the ball from side to side
And blew it back and forth.
Round in circles a hippo ran,
Turning and spinning about,
Until he dove and caught the ball
And the umpire yelled, "YOU'RE OUT!"

Now the game was over.
The victory was sealed.
All the jungle creatures cheered
The hippos on the field.

What a celebration
Of hippo glory, hippo fame
For the proud, triumphant winners
Of the jungle baseball game!

"Whacka, whacka, hoo boy,
Tie 'em with a rope.

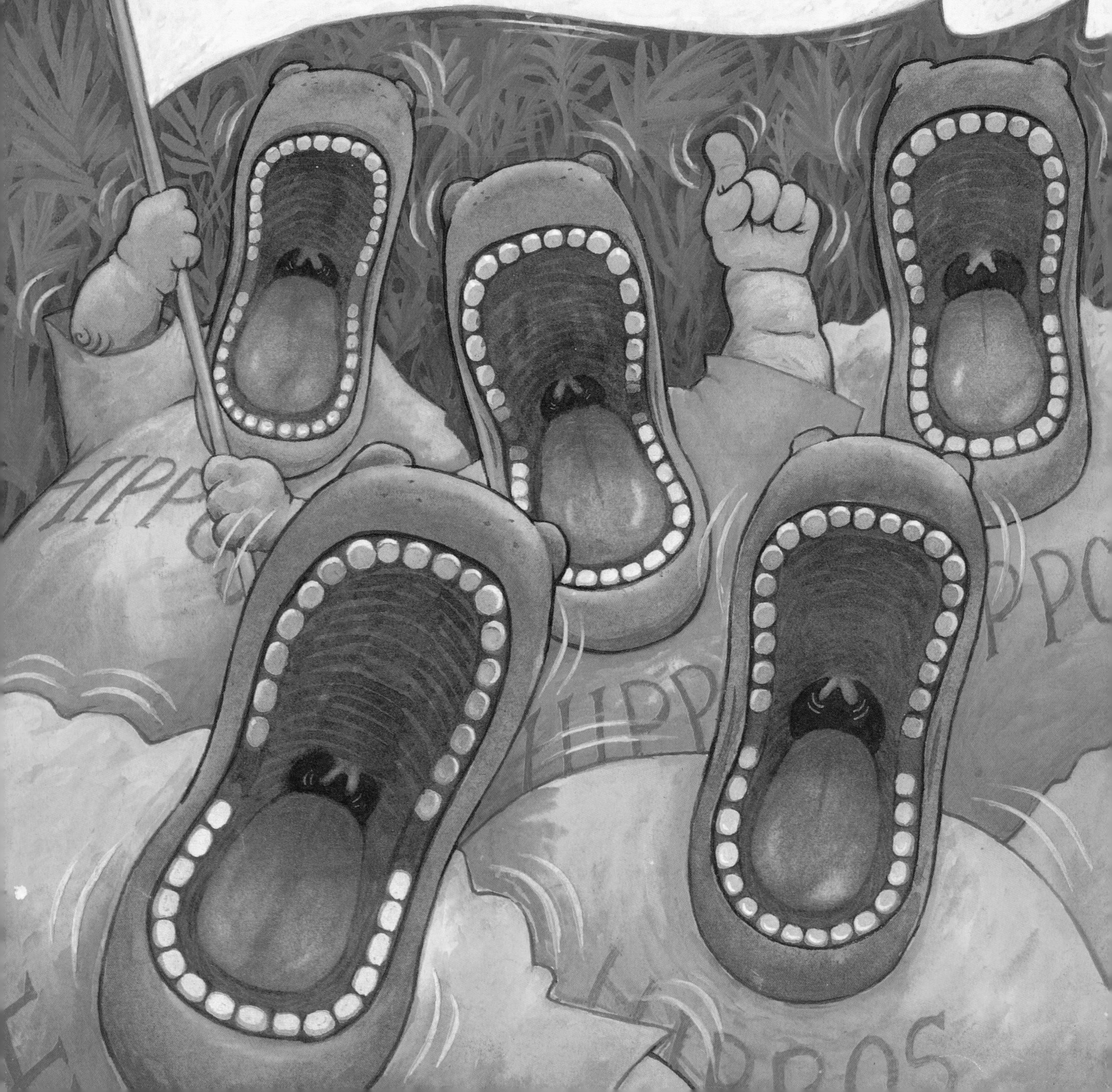

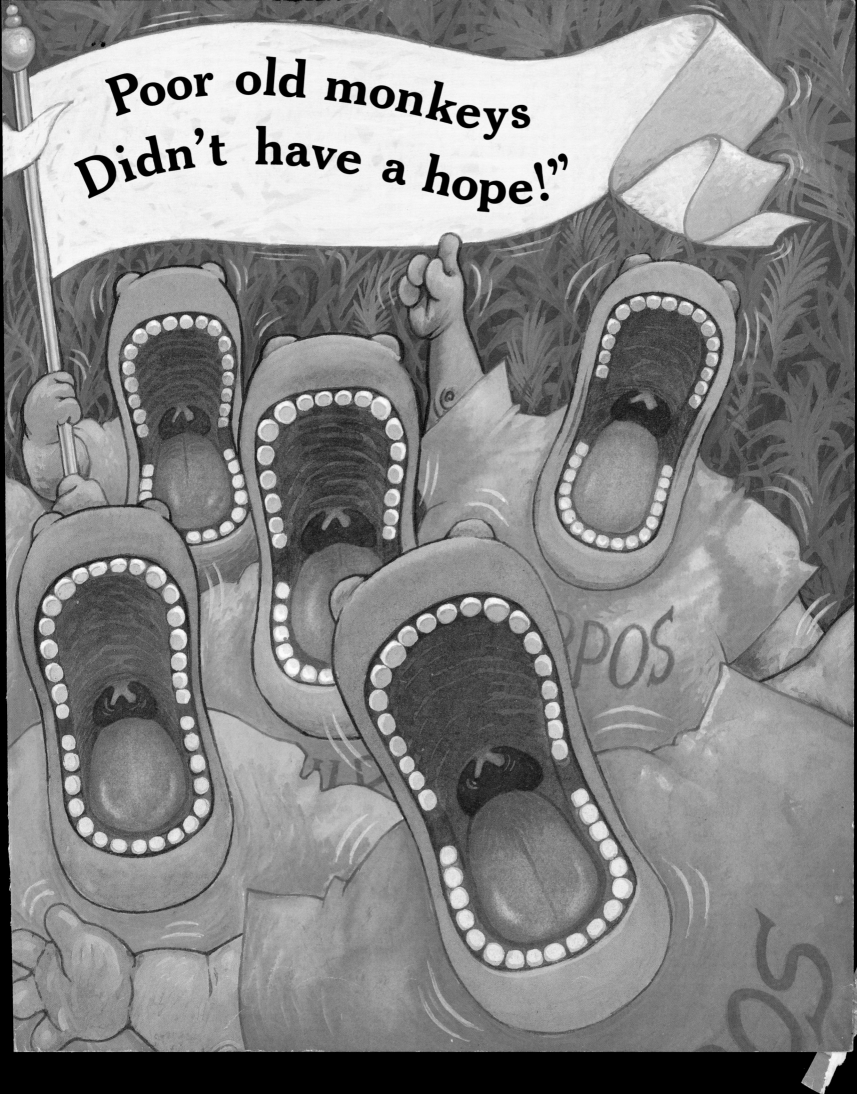

The Jungle Baseball Game

by TOM PAXTON

Brightly

Verse:

1. Rang - a - lang - lang, the tel - e - phone rang, way up in the co - co - nut tree. Mis - ter Mon - key ran to ans - wer: "Some-one's call - ing me." Mis - ter Hip - po, on the line, yelled, "Am I get - ting through? Get your mon - key base - ball team: We want to play ball with you." (Instrumental interlude)

2. When the mon - keys saw the hip - pos,